A Birthday on the Cowboy Ranch

Book 4

The Cowboy Ranch Series

Cover Photo:

Kim Stone Photography

Edited by: Lindsay Boone

*The events depicted int this book are purely fictitious. Any similarity to any person or persons is merely coincidental.**

This book is dedicated to my friend, Kathy Neuville and her beautiful Golden Retrievers. Without your support and love, this book would never have been written. Thank you for the many hours of barn time.

To Ruby ~ (yes, she IS real) Thank you for inspiring me to tell your story. Because of a beautiful, old dog, I learned that it's never too late to have a dream come true.

To Clem and Huck ~ I love your imagination and your encouragement!

To my family ~ Thank you for loving me.

A Birthday On The Cowboy Ranch

The Cowboy Ranch Series

Chapter 1

Saturday morning in Stone County was the best day of the week. All of the local folks met down by the old train station to buy and sell their fresh fruits and vegetables at the Farmer's Market.

Some people brought produce to sell, others came to buy, and some just came to talk and visit with their neighbors.

Clint Cowboy loved Saturday mornings. He got to see his best friend, Will Carpenter. Will lived on the next ranch over with his parents and his older sister, Lou.

Clint didn't get to see Will except at the Farmer's Market. Will and Lou were homeschooled by their mama. They sure made up for it on Saturday mornings, though.

Mama Cowboy had barely stopped the truck when Clint flung open the door and took off towards the crowd, looking for his friend. It didn't take Clint long to find Will.

They grabbed each other and rolled around on the ground, play fighting like they hadn't seen each other in years, instead of just a week.

Today was an extra special Saturday for Clint Cowboy. It was his birthday. Finally, he'd be 7, just like Will. "It's my birthday, Will. Did you remember? Now, I'm 7 just like you." With that, the two little boys were off to play, shoving each other about every other step.

Their laughter rang out as they ran towards the market square. Mama Cowboy smiled to herself as she finished setting her homemade pies on the table.

Clint had no idea that all of their friends were coming over to the ranch for ice cream and cake later that day. Mama Cowboy had told everyone that they were having a surprise birthday party for Clint. She knew her son.

He'd be telling all the town folks himself that it was his birthday, trying to get some of their pies and cookies. She didn't want him to have a full tummy, and she wanted him to be surprised.

Sure enough, Clint and Will made their rounds around the market square. They'd make their way up to each table and wait for the customers to finish talking. Clint would say, "Morning. It's my birthday." He'd step back and smile his best snaggle-toothed smile.

He just knew somebody would give him a slice or two of pie, but, so far, all he had gotten were lots of hugs and a bunch of old, sloppy kisses from the grandmas of the town.

This wasn't how it was supposed to work at all. Will stayed clear of those kissing grandmas. He was about to wonder if maybe they needed a bath or something. Why, they hadn't even gotten a cookie.

Mama Cowboy watched the two boys coming across the lawn towards her. Those were two of the saddest looking seven year olds she'd ever seen. Clint looked up at his mama with eyes the color of the summer sky.

"Mama, I've told everybody here that it's my birthday, and not one person even gave us a cookie. Is this what happens when you're 7, Mama? You get too old to get cookies for your birthday? 'Cause if it is, then I don't want to be 7 anymore," Clint declared.

Will looked over at his friend and elbowed him in the ribs. They both knew they weren't supposed to be asking for cookies or pies. Now Clint had done it!

Will just bet they were going to get in trouble. He looked up at Mama Cowboy with his best sad face and said, "Mrs. Cowboy, Clint just said it was his birthday. He didn't ask for nothing. Honest."

The boys were surprised when Mama Cowboy handed them both a big chocolate chip cookie. Maybe they wouldn't starve to death after all! The boys yelled their thanks as they took off towards the creek.

Chapter 2

The morning passed quickly, and soon it was time to pack up and head back to the ranch. Mama Cowboy had quickly sold everything off her table, leaving her with time to visit with her friends.   She spent a little extra time visiting with Mr. Wesley Thomas.

Mr. Wesley had recently moved to Stone County after losing his wife, Mrs. Mary. Mr. Wesley and Mrs. Mary had been married for over 50 years when Mrs. Mary got sick and went to Heaven. Although Mr. Wesley now lived with his son and family, he just couldn't seem to find his way.

Mama Cowboy made sure to invite the Thomas family out to the ranch for the birthday party, thinking that an afternoon of fun may cheer up Mr. Wesley.

Around lunch time, everyone started to pack up their tables to go home. Mama Cowboy turned towards the creek, stuck her thumb and finger in her mouth, and let loose with a whistle so loud that it caused an echo to bounce off the nearby buildings.

The whistle had barely ended when Clint appeared beside the truck, out of breath. He knew his mama meant business when she whistled for them. It didn't matter where they were, either. The Cowboy men recognized that whistle!

Clint Cowboy grabbed the last of the boxes and shoved them in the back seat of the truck, then climbed in and buckled his seatbelt. Mama Cowboy gave a wave and a wink to her friends and headed towards the ranch.

She looked over at Clint. He was fast asleep already. That boy could fall asleep quicker than anybody. Sleep was good, though. He'd need to rest up for his surprise.

Mama Cowboy drove extra slow to give everybody time to get to the ranch. Clint never stirred until they were bumping along the long driveway into the ranch.

He stretched and yawned, then sat straight up in the seat! What was going on? Why were all those trucks in his yard? Was that Grandpa and Grandma's truck?

He looked at his mama, and she was grinning at him! "Happy birthday, Clint," she said.

Clint bounced across the truck and landed in his mama's lap, nearly squeezing her neck off with a hug! Suddenly, being 7 was fun again. He was having a party!

Daddy Cowboy and Clint's big brother, Cody, had stayed home from the market this morning.

They pitched in to get the chores done and get everything ready for the party. They had the ice cream churn going on the porch.

Grandma was bringing out a cake when Clint ran up the steps. He knew what kind of cake it was, too. Grandma was known far and wide for her homemade strawberry birthday cakes. Clint wasn't disappointed.

Otis, the big White English bulldog, was running in circles, while Gibbs, the old fat beagle, was howling and wagging so hard he was dusting the ground with his fat belly. The ranch dogs loved a good party.

Chapter 3

Clint was so excited to see all of his friends at the ranch. He looked around the yard. There were his grandparents, Hank Welder and his parents, Sarah Rose and her mama, and the Carpenters.

Even his newest cousin, Tommy was there. Tommy was only a year old, but he was so much fun already. He toddled over to Clint and held up his chubby arms to be picked up, grinning the whole way.

Lou Carpenter, Will's 10 year old sister, started singing "Happy Birthday" in her sweet voice. Everyone joined in!

The Cowboy Family had a tradition for birthdays. They asked everyone to bring something useful for the community. Presents were nice, but they were usually forgotten. This year, all of the friends had brought books for the school library.

Clint looked at the big stack of colorful books and grinned that snaggle-toothed grin again. He told every person "thank you."

He could hardly contain himself as he ran around the table. Finally, he just blurted out, "Mama, I've been so good. It's my birthday. Can we please eat that strawberry cake and have some ice cream?"

Grandma began to cut the cake, giving Clint the first piece. Cody helped out by handing out the plates. He noticed Mr. Wesley sitting alone in the swing. Cody grabbed two plates of cake and ice cream and plopped down beside him. "I sure am glad you came out to the ranch, Mr. Wesley," Cody said.

As he handed a plate and fork to the old man, Cody started the swing to moving in a gentle sway. Sometimes, you didn't have to talk to be good company. Sometimes, you just had to be there.

After a while, Mr. Wesley started to ask questions about the ranch. Cody took his time with the old man. Even though all of the kids were running and playing games in the yard, Cody didn't hurry. They talked about the new calves and the crops.

Cody told him about the Stone County Fair and showing steers. Before long, Mr. Wesley had launched into an animated story of going hunting as a child. He described his hunting dog in such detail that Cody could almost see the golden dog running across the field to bring back a pheasant that had been shot. "Her name was Annie," the old man said.

This was the first time Cody had seen Mr. Wesley smile since he had met him. His heart lit up some. He was happy to see that smile.

They finished off their cake and ice cream, talking a little more. Cody noticed Mr. Wesley beginning to nod off. He gently took the empty plate from the old man's hand and eased out of the swing.

A good nap did sound mighty fine, but Cody reckoned he better go see what kind of trouble his little brother was into.

Chapter 4

The rest of the afternoon was filled with games and laughter. Even Ol' Boloney got in on some of the fun when he ran through the middle of the game of Duck, Duck, Goose. Boloney was the black and white pony that lived on the ranch. He could get out of any gate ever made. All of the children laughed when the pony came trotting by. Boloney was a legend in these parts.

The adults sat on the big, wide porch and watched the children run and play. Otis was right in the middle of the fun. It was pretty hard to play a game of ball when the bulldog was faster than all of the children. Otis would grab the ball and take off at a run. Then the chase was on!

Otis would get right in front of Clint, drop the ball on the ground, and wait. Clint would almost get the ball in his hand, and Otis would grab it and be gone again.

Usually, Gibbs kept watch from the top step of the porch. Daddy Cowboy thought it was strange that the old, fat beagle wasn't near the food. He never missed a meal. He was just about to go look for Gibbs when Otis ran by him with Clint hot on his heels.

Daddy Cowboy grabbed Clint in a big hug. Oh, my goodness. Clint was extra stinky today. Daddy Cowboy called Will over to him and hugged him, too. Yeah, Buddy. These boys were smelly.

Daddy Cowboy grabbed one boy in each arm and headed toward the watering trough. The boys were giggling, squirming, and doing their best to get free. Daddy Cowboy held both boys upside down over the water while they squealed with laughter.

All of a sudden, dead minnows and other little fish started to fall out of the boy's pockets.

It seems that while they were playing by the creek this morning, they caught a bunch of little fish. Clint and Will didn't have a place to put the fish, so they thought they'd just stuff them in their jeans pockets and get them out later. No wonder these two boys were smelly!

Daddy Cowboy dropped the boys into the trough with a big splash. They came up soaking wet and laughing. The two boys scrambled out of the water and took off running towards Sarah Rose and Lou.

The girls ran towards the barn, squealing like girls do. They were going to hide in the hay to keep Clint and Will from finding them.

Both girls slid to a stop in the doorway. They had stopped so fast that the boys thumped into their backs.Lou whispered, "Clint, go get your mom Hurry!" Clint took off in a run.

There in the hay stood Gibbs standing guard over the most pitiful looking dog the girls had ever seen. They tried to get closer to see, but Gibbs blocked the way. A low rumble came from the poor, scared stray dog. She quivered with fright, her eyes weary and tired. Between her paws lay a puppy, his fur still wet from his birth. He was so tiny and frail.

Chapter 5

Mama Cowboy saw Clint barrel up the steps of the porch, out of breath. He ran to her and grabbed her hand. "Mama, come quick. There's a dog in our hay, and she is sick, Mama. She has blood all over her head, and she is so sad. Hurry, Mama! Hurry!"

Mama Cowboy followed her son out to the barn. Everyone wanted to follow along, but, all of a sudden, Mr. Wesley stood up and took charge.

He said, "The last thing that poor dog needs is a bunch of people gawking at it. Everyone just sit back down and eat some cake. I'll go help them if they need it."

With that, he was down the steps and heading to the barn. Everybody was kind of shocked, especially Joey Thomas, Mr. Wesley's son. Maybe there was some life left in his dad after all.

Mr. Wesley slipped through the barn door in time to see Mama Cowboy ease down on the hay near Gibbs. The old beagle still stood between Mama Cowboy and the poor battered dog crouching in the corner.

Mr. Wesley whispered to the children to go on back out and play. The children started to argue, but the look Mr. Wesley gave them had them scattering like quail.

Mr. Wesley eased his way over to the hay. Again, a low growl came from the dog. Gibbs wagged his tail and licked the stray's face, as if to say that these humans were ok.

Mr. Wesley told Mama Cowboy to help him sit down on a bale of hay. Another sharp look cut off the protest Mama Cowboy was about to make. She helped the old man ease his way down onto a nearby bale.

"Go fetch me some water and some of that chicken you fried up for the boy. Pull it off the bone. Not too much now. She doesn't look like she's had a meal in a long time."

Mr. Wesley dismissed Mama Cowboy and gently turned to the dog. If possible, the poor girl had backed even further into the corner. He could see that her fur was matted and bloody. She had a haunted look in her eyes.

He raised his hand to touch her, and she cowered over her baby. Gibbs instantly bumped Mr. Wesley's hand down, letting him know that was close enough.

The old man began to pet Gibbs, talking to him gently. He rubbed his ears and face. He leaned over as best as he could and rubbed his face on the old beagle's face; then he turned the beagle towards the stray and gently pushed him towards her.

The stray sniffed Gibbs' face, taking in the scent of the old man. Gibbs again licked her head, gently trying to clean her wounds.

This went on for a few minutes. Mr. Wesley kept calling the beagle to him, petting him and loving him, while he spoke softly. Then he'd send him back to the stray.

When Mama Cowboy came into the barn with the water and food, she was surprised to see the stray out of the corner. "Set it down here and leave us. I'll call you if I need you," Mr. Wesley whispered.

Mama Cowboy smiled to herself as she did as she was told. Not too many people bossed Mama Cowboy around and got away with it. She knew something special was happening here.

Chapter 6

Outside of the barn, the birthday celebration had come to a stop. Mama Cowboy gathered everybody around and told them what was going on in the barn.

Daddy Cowboy said, "Well, we were going to do some fishing and have a campfire a little later on. Why don't we all go on down to the lake now? Mama, could you get the marshmallows?"

Excited chatter broke out as the children ran towards the water. The men gathered up their fishing poles and followed them.

After cleaning up the porch and covering the food, the ladies grabbed the marshmallows and headed down to the lake to join the rest of the party.

As they passed the barn door, Mama Cowboy peeked inside. There sat Mr. Wesley with Gibbs asleep at his feet on one side and the poor battered stray and her pup resting on the other.

Mama Cowboy could see that she was a golden red color. Mr. Wesley was gently stroking the stray's head.

Mama Cowboy had to hold back tears as she heard the old man say, "Old Girl, I think I will call you 'Ruby.' You'll be beautiful again soon. And, I know how you feel. Being alone is a bad place to be. I reckon we belong together now. God must have known I needed you, and you sure needed me."

Mama Cowboy slipped back out of the barn and walked down to the lake. There would be no question about what they should do with the stray. All they would need to do would be to convince Gibbs. He had always been the protector of strays around these parts.

Before that thought could clear her mind, she felt one of the bags of marshmallows get yanked from her hand. A flash of black and white fuzz took off at a run across the pasture, marshmallows flying. Boloney!

That pony was out again. Mama Cowboy guessed it was too quiet in the barn for his ornery old hide, so he decided he should escape and join in the fun.

She laughed as she watched the pony eating a sticky marshmallow, his nose curling up and his teeth shining.

She reached the lake just in time to see Clint and Will light into each other like two wet cats in a sack. She would have thought they were fighting, but she knew what was about to happen.

She took off at a run towards the two boys! Mama Cowboy wasn't fast enough, though.

Splash! Clint hit the water first, then Will. Clint came up, sputtering and spitting, claiming he'd never got washed two times in the same day.

Laughter sounded across the meadow as the rest of the children jumped in the lake. Daddy Cowboy looked over at Henry Welder and said, "Well, I guess there goes the fishing."

Chapter 7

Daddy and Mama Cowboy sat together with their friends, watching the children play and laugh. It had been a wonderful day.

After a while, Mr. Wesley made his way across the pasture to join them.

"She's sleeping now," he said as he took a chair beside his son. "I reckon I don't want to leave her, Joey. She needs me," he said.

Joey looked at his wife. She winked at him and gave a soft nod. In a gruff voice, so as not to show the emotion, Joey said, "I figured as much. I've already been thinking on how we could get her home."

Mr. Wesley reached over laid his weathered, old hand on Joey's shoulder. "Give me a stick and some marshmallows, Son. You still like them a little burned, right?"

For the first time since they had lost their wife and mother, the Thomas men smiled a real smile, one that reached all the way to their eyes.

Way too soon, the evening was over. As friends made their way back to the house to gather up their belongings, Clint and Will headed towards the gate by the barn. The boys were so tired that they could hardly shove each other, but they still gave it a half-hearted effort.

Boloney stood by the gate, waiting for his supper. Will asked, "Reckon how he can get out of any gate, but he can't get back in?"

Clint answered, "That's just 'cause he 'chievious, Will. Like us."

Cody and Hank Welder had started feeding the barn horses by the time Clint and Will got Boloney back in his stall.

Sarah Rose and Lou were helping out by making sure all of the horses had fresh water.

The friends made quick work of their chores and headed to the house, Otis between them. Gibbs met them about halfway through the barn.

The old dog was jumping and spinning around, wagging his tail like crazy. Why, he looked plum proud of himself.

When the friends got to the front of the barn, where the hay was kept, they could see why Gibbs was so excited. Mr. Wesley, cradling the new pup tenderly in his arms, was making his way out to his truck. Walking so close she was touching him, was the stray.

The friends stood watching as Joey opened the truck door; the stray jumped right in, and then she turned and waited for Mr. Wesley and her pup to climb in. She settled right down with a contented sigh, her head resting on Mr. Wesley's knee.

Yes sir, this was one birthday that wouldn't soon be forgotten in Stone County. The Cowboy family agreed that there was no place they'd rather be than right here on this ranch.

Epilogue

Spring turned into summer and summer into fall. Life went on just like it always did in Stone County.

People came to town for the Farmer's Market on Saturdays, only now there were two new faces to see. Ruby had, indeed, become a beautiful dog under Mr. Wesley's care.

Turns out, Ruby and her son were Golden Retrievers. Her coat shined like a new penny in the sun. Ruby was totally devoted to Mr. Wesley, rarely leaving his side.

The pup, which the Thomas family had named Finn, now he was a different story. He was beautiful and smart, but he hadn't quite learned that not everybody wanted all of their belongings "retrieved."

Clint and Will made it their "job" to return papers, hats, and balls to the rightful owners at the market. After all, they knew that Finn was just 'chievious, just like them.

~ Ruby and Finn ~

87480163R00022

Made in the USA
Columbia, SC
28 January 2018